THE RUNAWAY RABBIT

CHRISTINE WOOD

Illustrations by
Jo Worth

LUTTERWORTH PRESS
CAMBRIDGE

Lutterworth Press
7 All Saints' Passage
Cambridge CB2 3LS

British Library Cataloguing in Publication Data

Wood, Chris, 1902–
The runaway rabbit.—(Junior gateway)
I. Title   II. Series
832'.914 [J]   PZ7

ISBN 0-7188-2680-9

Typeset in Monophoto Century Schoolbook by
Vision Typesetting, Manchester
Printed in Great Britain by
The Guernsey Press Co. Ltd.,
Guernsey, Channel Islands.

THE RUNAWAY RABBIT

Susie has entrusted the care of her rabbit to Andrew, making him promise not to let it out of the hutch. Andrew breaks his promise and the rabbit escapes. His efforts to recapture it teach him some of the important lessons of Christian living.

JUNIOR GATEWAY BOOKS

CONTENTS

1

Oh, For a Rabbit!

ANDREW Miller pressed his nose against the kitchen window. He looked down on the patch of grass where his friend Susie kept her rabbit hutch. He could see the white rabbit hopping round its wire-netted run.

"Mum, I wish I could have a rabbit like Susie's," Andrew sighed.

He turned towards his mother who was scraping potatoes at the sink. She popped a small round one into a saucepan and picked up another.

"I'd like you to have a rabbit, dear, but you know we've nowhere to keep it," she said.

"It's not fair. I'm eight and I still haven't got a pet. Susie's only seven and she's had that rabbit for ages," Andrew went on.

"Susie can keep a rabbit because ground-floor flats have small gardens. When we can move to somewhere with a garden you can certainly have a rabbit," Mum promised.

"And when will that be?" Andrew asked, his brown eyes hopeful.

"I don't know. We're on the council waiting list for a bigger home . . . Oh dear, there's Lucy crying. Be a good boy and talk to her while I get her feed ready," Mum said.

"What's the use of talking to her? She can't talk back," Andrew replied, and he sounded as grumpy as he felt.

"It would be helpful if you would obey without arguing. Please see if you can stop Lucy from crying. We don't want Miss Pritt complaining again," Mum said.

She pushed back the hair that kept falling round her face and put the saucepan on the cooker.

"I wish Lucy was a white rabbit," Andrew muttered.

"You silly boy, white rabbits can't talk either," Mum said, smiling. "Lift Lucy out of her cot and put her on the floor, will you?"

Andrew's little sister stopped crying almost as soon as he sat her on the carpet. He knelt down beside her and wiped her wet cheeks with his hanky. He also made funny faces at her.

Lucy gurgled, then lay down and kicked her fat little legs in the air. Andrew was still playing with her when the front doorbell rang.

"I'll go," he shouted.

He opened the door and saw Susie on the landing. Her hair hung over her eyes and she had a door-key dangling from a string round her neck. She smiled a watery smile and sniffed at the same time.

"You look as if you've been crying, like my sister," Andrew said.

"I have a bit," Lucy replied. "Can you play with me? My mummy isn't home yet and I don't like being on my own."

She sniffed again and Andrew asked her to come in.

"Mum, it's Susie. Can I go and play with her?" Andrew asked.

"Not now, dear. Dad will be home in a minute. Will you please put the knives and forks on the table while I give Lucy her bottle?" Mum said.

"But I don't want to lay the table. I'd much rather play with Susie," Andrew said.

"Please do as I ask without arguing," Mum replied.

She picked Lucy up and put the feeding bottle in her mouth. Susie stood in the doorway watching. She also sniffed and wiped her eyes with her hair.

"My daddy doesn't come home any more. He's gone away and Mummy has to work to keep us," she said.

She looked so sad that Andrew put his arm round her and kissed her wet cheek.

"I'm very sorry, dear," Mum said.

"It's Saturday tomorrow so Andrew can play with you after breakfast."

"Hello there! Nice to have the front door open to welcome me," a man's voice called.

"Hello, Dad," Andrew said.

His father kissed Mum and the baby and ruffled Andrew's thick, wavy hair. He then went to wash his hands ready for tea, and Andrew quickly laid the table. He knew they were having salad and new potatoes and remembered to put out the salad cream.

"You are lucky having your dad," Susie said to him, and she ran from the flat before he could reply.

"That poor child, having to come home to an empty flat. She must come up here after school in future," Mum said.

"Oswald Chop jeers at her at school and calls her the Latchkey Kid because of that key dangling down," Andrew replied.

"How horrid! I hope you don't tease her so unkindly," Mum said.

"Of course I don't. Susie's my friend," Andrew protested.

At bedtime he was putting on his pyjamas when Dad came in and sat on the bed. It was such a tiny room he had nowhere else to sit.

"Mum tells me that you've been arguing again today and have disobeyed her," Dad said.

Andrew slid between the sheets and shut his eyes. He hated it when his father had to speak to him about bad behaviour.

"You told me that you had put your trust in Jesus at Sunday School, and that you wanted to be a better boy," Dad continued.

"Yes, I told Jesus I was sorry for the wrong things I've done ... and yet sometimes it's still easy to do wrong things," Andrew blurted out.

"Let's ask Jesus to help you to obey,

shall we?" Dad suggested.

Andrew liked listening to Dad talking to Jesus. But inside himself he knew that he also still liked having his own way.

Andrew lay awake for some time watching the odd shadows that the setting sun cast on the bedroom wall. He thought about Susie and how horrid it must be now that her dad had gone away.

"I'm lucky to have a mum and dad who really care about me," he whispered. "Please, Jesus, bless Susie and help her not to mind being called the Latchkey Kid."

2

The Runaway

ANDREW awoke to the sound of rain beating on the windows.

"Never mind, it's Saturday and next week is half-term holiday," he said and jumped out of bed.

After breakfast he was just going down to Susie's when his mother asked him to dry the dishes.

"But Mum . . ." he began, then remembered what Dad had said about arguing and being disobedient.

He pulled the tea-towel off the line and dried the breakfast things without saying a word.

"Thank you, that's a big help," Mum said, and she looked pleased.

Andrew went down the iron steps at the back of the flats to Susie's. When he wore his winter shoes the heels made a nice loud clonk on the steps. But today was a showery spring day and the trainers he wore made no sound.

"Oh well, Miss Pritt can't grumble at me for making a noise," Andrew said to himself.

Susie's mother opened the back door when he knocked. Her hair looked untidy and she wore a faded blue dressing-gown.

"Come on in, love," she said, puffing cigarette smoke into his face. "It's too wet to play outside but you kids can draw at the kitchen table while I do the hoovering."

"I'll clean out Percy's hutch when it stops raining," Susie said.

"I'll help you," Andrew offered eagerly.

"I know what, I'll bring him indoors. Mummy lets me bring him in sometimes 'cos he can't move much in his run. He likes hopping round the kitchen."

"You should let him run on the

16

grass," Andrew said.

"I daren't. He ran away once and Mummy had a job catching him," Susie replied.

She ran outside and lifted the white rabbit from his hutch. He wriggled in her arms but she held him tight.

"He's not used to you," Susie said to Andrew, who knelt on the kitchen floor to watch Percy hopping round the table and chairs.

"He doesn't mind me now," he said.

"Come on, let's draw him," Susie replied. "Mummy gets this big paper from work. It's scrap paper but I like drawing on it."

They had not been drawing long when Andrew jumped.

"Ouch! Something hit my knee!" he exclaimed, and Susie giggled.

"It's only Percy. He sits up on his back legs and bangs you with his front paw when he wants to be friends," she said.

Andrew forgot about drawing after

that. He knelt on the floor again and the white rabbit let him stroke its silky ears and soft, furry coat.

"If only I could have a rabbit!" he sighed.

"You'd need a hutch and a wire run to keep it in," Susie said. "Daddy made my hutch and . . ."

Her voice caught in a sort of sob and Andrew thought she was going to cry.

"Well, that's the hoovering done. I'm gasping for a cup of coffee," Susie's mother said, pushing the vacuum cleaner into a cupboard.

Andrew noticed that she had also changed into a dress and combed her hair. It made her look different, more like his own mum.

"That sounded like the postman. See what he's brought, Susie," her mother said as she put the kettle on.

Susie came back with two brown envelopes and a pale blue one. Her mother tossed the brown envelopes on to the table, but opened the blue one at once.

"Listen to this, Susie love," she said a minute later. "Gran says you can stay with her for the half-term holiday next week. She says to take you over tomorrow."

"Goody! Goody!" Susie exclaimed. "I'd much rather go to Gran's than have that fussy Miss Pritt look after me."

"What about your rabbit?" Andrew asked.

"Mummy will look after him," Susie said.

"Look, love, supposing you and I do it between us?" her mother said to Andrew. "I'm not much of a one with animals but I'll feed him when I get home from work if you'll keep his hutch clean and give him fresh water each morning."

"I'd love that!" Andrew said.

And so it was arranged. The rain had stopped and Susie took Andrew into the garden to show him exactly what to do.

"I shall pretend Percy belongs to me," he said.

"You needn't pretend. He's yours until I come home but you must take care of him," Susie replied.

"Listen, love, be sure not to take that creature from his hutch. You'll never catch him if he runs away," Susie's mother said.

"All right, I'll just sit on the grass and talk to him through the netting," Andrew replied.

And that is what he did on Sunday afternoon after Susie's mother had taken her to her gran's. The rabbit looked at him through the wire netting and he put his finger inside to stroke his soft nose.

"You're mine, my very own until Susie comes home," he said, and the rabbit twitched his pink nose.

After that the rabbit hopped close to the netting whenever he saw Andrew

coming. By Wednesday morning they were good friends. He was cleaning out the hutch when Susie's mother shouted to him on her way to work.

"I'm fetching Susie home tomorrow afternoon, love," she said, "so you won't have to do that chore any more."

"It isn't a chore. I like looking after Percy," Andrew called back.

He had a sick, lonely feeling because the rabbit would soon be Susie's again.

On Thursday morning he went down to see Percy as soon as he had dried the breakfast things. As usual the rabbit poked his twitching, pink nose through the netting to greet him.

Andrew slid back the bolts that kept the top netting in place. He put his arm inside so he could stroke all of Percy, not just his nose. But even that was not enough. He longed to have him on his lap and hold him in his arms.

"You're mine for the very last day," he said.

The rabbit looked up at him, his long ears alert. Andrew became more and more churned up inside. Part of him badly wanted to lift Percy out, but another part of him remembered that Susie's mother had warned him not to.

He wondered if Jesus would be sorry to see him doing something someone else's mother had told him not to.

Perhaps it was not as bad as disobeying his own mother.

"Surely it wouldn't matter if I just held him on my lap," Andrew muttered, weakening.

Just then Percy stood up on his hind legs to sniff at the hand resting on the netting. Andrew could resist no longer. He opened the top wide and lifted the rabbit out. A warm glow of pleasure surged through him as Percy settled on his lap.

"You're mine right now," Andrew told him. "How would you like it if . . ."

He never finished that sentence. A motorbike roared away from a nearby garage and the terrified rabbit bolted. It reached the fence in a few bounds, shot underneath and ran on to some waste ground.

"Stop! Stop!" Andrew yelled.

He ran to the fence, which was only two strands of wire fixed to posts. He lay down flat and rolled underneath the wire, then scrambled to his feet. It horrified him to see the white rabbit running towards the road on the right.

Percy looked like a big cotton wool ball springing and bouncing across the uneven ground. Andrew raced after him.

The rabbit ran across the road towards the council tip and a driver braked hard to avoid hitting him. By the time Andrew could cross the road Percy had disappeared.

Usually Andrew liked exploring on that rubbish dump. He had found all kinds of treasures, including a bicycle pump and a wooden fort which his dad had repainted to look like new.

Once he had found a doll's pram which he thought Lucy would like when she was bigger, but Mum had told him to take it back to the dump.

"You never know where things like that have been," she had said.

She had also told Andrew not to go on

the council tip any more, but now he was too upset to remember that. And he wanted to find only one treasure – Susie's white rabbit.

At last he saw him! The rabbit had stopped running and was sniffing round a pile of rags. Andrew crept towards him on tiptoe. Suddenly he sprang and his fingers sank into the rabbit's thick fur. Percy rolled over, kicked hard, and was off in a flash.

Andrew lay on his stomach and groaned. How was he going to catch Susie's rabbit? He jumped up and looked all round but Percy had vanished again amongst the rubble.

Andrew hardly knew whether to run or creep about in the hope of catching the rabbit unawares.

He heard something rumbling towards him. He looked round and saw a bulldozer. He dodged out of its path and ran across the tip.

"Hey, you! What are you doing on

council property? Do you want to be flattened by that bulldozer?" someone shouted.

Andrew saw a big, burly man in a red check shirt standing in the doorway of a wooden hut.

"I've lost a rabbit," Andrew shouted.

"A racket?" the man boomed above the bulldozer's clatter.

"No, a rabbit, a live one," Andrew replied, running closer.

The man scratched his bushy hair with a fat finger and stared at Andrew.

"Well, lad, you'll find no live rabbit on that there tip and that's for sure," he said. "Young Harry will soon make mincemeat of it with that bulldozer."

"It was alive just now and I almost caught it," Andrew argued.

The man shaded his eyes, then shook his head.

"No rabbits round here. You'd better give up and get off this tip," the man said. "Sorry I can't help you."

"I can't give up! I must find him . . . he's my friend's rabbit," Andrew panted.

"Well, let your friend find his own rabbit," the man said. "You kids are a menace grubbing around on this tip. The notice says 'KEEP OFF' plain enough. No sense of danger, that's your trouble."

Andrew turned away. What could he do next?

3

The Long Chase

ANDREW crossed the road again.
"Perhaps that bulldozer's frightened Percy back here," he muttered.

He stood on an old milk crate and looked all round but could not see the white rabbit. The sound of sawing and hammering reached him from the far end of the waste ground. He could see builders working on the new council houses. Could Percy be hiding there?

Andrew went nearer and saw a lot of hiding places on the building site – stacks of wood, a concrete mixer and piles of bricks. Broken tiles and other rubble lay all over the ground. As Andrew stared at it all he felt more and more helpless.

"Percy could be hiding anywhere!

Absolutely anywhere!" he exclaimed.

He paused in his search to watch a small lift taking tiles up to a new roof.

"What yer looking at, sonny?" one of the builders asked. "Like as not you'll get something landing on yer head if yer hang around here, so watch it."

"I'm looking for a white rabbit," Andrew told him.

"A white rabbit! Yer've got to be joking," the builder replied.

"No, he's a real, live rabbit and I've lost him," Andrew said. "He might be hiding in one of these houses."

"If yer wants to search yer'd better ask the foreman first 'cos yer's trespassing, see?" the builder said, and climbed up a nearby ladder.

Andrew wandered on.

"He's over there," the builder shouted, jerking his thumb towards an aluminium hut.

Andrew found the foreman drinking a mug of tea inside the hut.

"Can I look for a lost rabbit in these houses?" he asked.

The foreman was friendly and helpful. He swallowed the last of his tea, then came out to look at the council houses.

"No good looking in that lot," he said, waving his arm to the left. "They've got no floorboards in so you'll break your neck climbing about in them."

They both searched in the nearly finished houses but the rabbit was nowhere to be seen.

"How come you lost the rabbit anyway?" the foreman asked.

"I had just taken him out of his run when a motorbike scared him and he ran away," Andrew explained.

He felt his face flush with guilt. It was a horrid feeling.

"I . . . I think I'd better have another search nearer the flats," he blurted out.

He ran off before the foreman could

ask any more questions. Half-way across the bumpy field Andrew slowed down. He watched a man with a brown and white dog walking along the back of the flats. Suddenly the dog yelped and raced off after . . . could it be? Yes, it was a white rabbit!

Andrew stumbled on the rough ground while the man whistled to his

dog. He picked himself up and ran after the dog. He could see the rabbit bounding towards a row of houses with gardens backing on to the field.

Percy shot through a hole in a fence and the dog yelped and clawed at the hole but was too big to get through. Andrew panted up, grabbed hold of the fence and hauled himself to the top. But a strand of barbed wire stopped him from climbing over. He tried to get one leg over it but got stuck.

"That's a silly thing to do. Don't you know you can't argue with barbed wire?" the dog owner said.

He hauled Andrew down. RIP! His jeans tore on the wire as the man pulled him away.

"I must get over there!" Andrew shouted above the dog's yelps.

"But it's a private garden," the man said. "Shut up, Ranter! And stop clawing at that fence," he added, grabbing his dog by the collar.

"That was my friend's rabbit your dog chased. I've been trying to catch him for ages," Andrew shouted.

"Well, calm down! Go round and ask at the front door if you can get the rabbit from the garden," the man said.

Andrew glanced along the row of houses. He saw the high church wall at the building site end and realised it would be quicker to go back to the flats to get round to the road.

He ran off, hoping that his mother would not see him and ask where he was going.

Once on the pavement, Andrew dashed down the road and round the corner into Park Avenue. Then he stopped and stared. In his hurry he had forgotten to count how many houses along the one he wanted was from the corner.

"I can't go knocking at all the doors!" he panted.

He was still standing there when

Trevor Cummings cycled towards him. Trevor was nine and in the class above him at school. He lived in the third house along.

"Can't you find your way home?" Trevor asked, a broad grin on his freckled face.

He braked and put one foot on to the ground, so Andrew poured out his story.

"The rabbit went into the garden with a hole in the fence. I'll have to go round the back and count to see which one it is," Andrew finished.

"What's the garden like? Only I've been in some near my house to get balls that I've sent flying," Trevor said.

"All I saw was rows of little plants near the fence and . . . and glass things with more plants under them," Andrew told him.

"Ah, now, that's a vital clue," said Trevor, who loved detective stories in books and on TV. "It sounds as if it could be Mr Gunter's garden. He's mad on growing things and gives my mum carrots and lettuces. Our house is number 3 so his must be number 6. I'm sure he's three doors along."

"Will you come with me?" Andrew asked.

Trevor leaned his bike against the wall of his own house, then showed Andrew where Mr Gunter lived.

"He's German and talks in a funny way," Trevor whispered as he rang the doorbell.

"Vat is it you boys vant?" Mr Gunter asked, peering at them through gold-rimmed spectacles. He had a loud deep voice although he was a thin little man.

"My friend's lost a rabbit. It got through a hole in your fence and it's in the back garden," Trevor said.

"A rabbit you say? Not a ball zis time?" Mr Gunter replied, rubbing his nose with a bony finger.

"Yes, a white rabbit. Can I get him, please?" Andrew asked.

They all trooped round the back and saw the rabbit nibbling at a row of small green plants.

"Ze vicked brute! He eat my lettuce plants!" Mr Gunter exclaimed.

The rabbit pricked up his ears. Next, he sat up, his pink nose twitching. Andrew crept forward to grab him but with one leap Percy disappeared through the hole in the fence.

"You slow clot! I could have caught him easily," Trevor said.

"Well you didn't, did you?" Andrew replied crossly.

"Zat brute eat much lettuce!" Mr Gunter complained, pointing and wringing his thin, bony hands.

"I'm ever so sorry," Andrew said.

"You catch zat vild beast on ze vaste ground. I block zat hole up so he come no more here," Mr Gunter replied.

Out on the pavement again, Andrew struggled against a feeling of dull despair.

"I've simply got to catch that rabbit. Susie's coming home this afternoon. Her dad's gone away for good and that's bad enough without her losing her rabbit as well," he blurted out.

To Trevor the whole thing was like a real-life detective story.

"We must both be spies and the rabbit must not suspect he is being watched," he said. "Come on, let's creep round the back and spy on him under cover."

Andrew could not think of any 'cover' but he ran round the corner with Trevor. The next moment he wanted to hide. Mum was wheeling Lucy towards him. She would be sure to ask awkward questions.

"Where *have* you been all the morning?" she wanted to know.

"I . . . I've been playing with Trevor," Andrew lied.

"You know you shouldn't go off without saying where you are going," Mum said.

"We have to keep things secret. Spies never reveal their movements," Trevor joined in.

"Well, secrets or not, come indoors now, Andrew," Mum said.

He and Trevor looked helplessly at each other.

"I'll keep going. Report to Base Three

when you can," Trevor whispered out of the side of his mouth.

Andrew was puzzled until he realised that Trevor meant him to come to his house in Park Avenue.

4

A Big Disappointment

ANDREW held the hall door open so that Mum could wheel Lucy into the block of flats. The milkman came towards them, whistling. He was carrying an empty crate so Andrew held the door open for him too.

"Thanks, young Andy," the milkman said.

Andrew hated being called Andy but he liked the friendly milkman.

"Fred, did you remember to leave me some orange juice?" Mum asked.

"Yes, ma'am," Fred replied.

Mum put the pram under the stairs and then carried Lucy up to their flat.

"Those stairs! I wish the council would give us a house," Mum grumbled, and she sounded out of breath.

Andrew took the milk and orange juice indoors and stood them on the draining board in the kitchen. He did not dare to tell Mum about Percy's escape. She would be angry with him for taking the rabbit from the run when he had been told not to.

He sneaked miserably into his bedroom and stared out of the window. He wondered what Trevor was doing, but could not see the waste ground from there. If he put his head out and looked up the road, all he could see was the edge of the park.

He left the window and sank on to his bed. He saw the Bible he had won as a Sunday School prize lying on a shelf. He picked it up to look at the pictures. Andrew liked the ones of Jesus best.

He spent a long time looking at a picture with the words "The Denial" underneath. It showed Jesus looking sadly at Peter as he warmed himself by a fire on a dark night.

Andrew knew the story. Although Peter was one of Jesus' closest friends, he denied three times that he even knew him.

Andrew turned back the pages and found another picture of Jesus as a boy of twelve. He was walking with his parents and wore a loose cotton robe down to his knees.

"It looks cooler than my jeans," Andrew thought.

He read the words under the picture: "Jesus lived in Nazareth, where he obeyed his parents."

"Perhaps he can help me to do what I'm told," Andrew whispered as he stroked the picture with his finger.

He thought of all the things that had gone wrong since he had taken the rabbit from his run. Should he tell Jesus about the trouble he was in?

"Will he help me when Percy's only lost because I would have my own way?" Andrew wondered. "Perhaps I should say I'm sorry first."

But before the words would come right, Andrew heard a crash. Mum cried out "Oh dear!" and he ran to her in the kitchen.

"Why didn't you put the milk in the fridge?" she asked. "Now I've knocked a bottle over."

Milk spread everywhere. It looked more like a bucketful than just one pint.

"It would happen when I've no spare milk, and it's nearly time for Lucy's feed," Mum said.

Andrew helped to wipe up the mess. It was then that Mum noticed the tear in his jeans.

"However did you do that?" she asked.

"I . . . I tripped on some barbed wire out the back," Andrew said.

"More mending! I wish you'd keep off that waste ground," Mum sighed.

Andrew rinsed out the cloth he had used to wipe the floor. He hoped Mum would not notice his red face. He could always feel his face going red when he told an untruth.

"I tell you what," Mum said. "Fred drives his milk-float down Park Avenue, then turns at the church and comes back. Will you run to the corner and wave to him to stop. Ask him for another pint of milk, please."

Andrew ran off, glad to help. He also hoped that he might see Trevor. He stood on the corner and looked down Park Avenue. Sure enough, the milk-float was coming towards him.

While he waited, Andrew looked across to the park opposite. There he saw Trevor speeding along on his bike.

"He's mean! He doesn't care about Susie's rabbit," he muttered.

Andrew felt all alone again in his search. He waved to Fred, who drew up at the kerb.

"You look glum today, young Andy. What's up?" Fred asked.

He looked so kind and friendly that Andrew blurted out his story.

"A white rabbit! D'you know what? When I took the vicarage milk in I spotted something white in the churchyard, honest I did," Fred said.

"Was it a rabbit?" Andrew asked breathlessly.

"Couldn't say for sure, I only got a glimpse, mind – but it was white and furry sure as nuts is nuts," Fred said. "Tell you what . . ."

But Andrew did not stop to listen. He ran all the way to the churchyard. He arrived just in time to see a golden weathercock being lowered to the ground on ropes. He had often looked at it high on the church steeple, where it seemed quite small. Now it looked huge.

The vicar stood nearby watching a man untie the weathercock. He smiled at Andrew.

"Hello, have you come to watch the

steeplejack?" he asked. "Here he comes!"

Andrew looked up and saw another man climbing down a long ladder.

"Why has he taken the cock down?" Andrew asked.

"It has to be repainted," the vicar told him, as the two men carried the cock away. "Do you know why we have a cock on the steeple?"

"To show which way the wind's blowing," Andrew said.

"Good, but there's also another reason," the vicar replied.

"I don't know," Andrew admitted.

"Ah well, I'm sure you know the Bible story about the apostle Peter," the vicar smiled.

"You mean when he boasted that he would never let Jesus down?" Andrew asked.

"That's right. It upset Peter when Jesus told him that before the cock crowed twice, he would have denied him three times," the vicar went on.

"Yet Peter did, didn't he?" Andrew said.

"Yes, after some soldiers had captured Jesus, three different people asked Peter if he knew him. Three times he said he didn't – then a cock crowed."

"What's that got to do with the cock on the steeple?" Andrew wanted to know.

"It's there to remind us that it grieves Jesus when we tell lies," the vicar said.

"I . . . I hope I'll remember," Andrew replied.

"Well now, I must get back to my study. I've decided to preach about Peter next Sunday," the vicar said, and off he went.

Andrew remembered he had come to the churchyard to find Percy. He looked about him, then went round the side of the church. All at once his heart beat faster. He could see something white lying in the sun among some flowers.

He crept forward, then nearly choked with disappointment. A snow-white cat lay curled up fast asleep.

"So that's what Fred saw!" Andrew exclaimed in disgust.

Half-way along Park Avenue he noticed three pints of milk on a doorstep. They reminded him of the milk he was supposed to get from Fred. He went hot and cold all over. Mum would be angry with him for forgetting.

He looked longingly at the milk on the doorstep. Dare he take a bottle? He glanced up and down the road. No one was in sight.

Andrew stood by the gate, his fingers hot and sticky on the latch.

"I can't do it! I mustn't steal!" he muttered.

His bottom lip trembled and the milk bottles became blurred white blobs. He dashed away a tear and ran home empty-handed.

"You've been a long time," Mum said.

"I . . . I've been waiting for Fred," Andrew replied in a wobbly voice.

"No milk? Oh dear, you must have missed him. Will you fetch a pint from the corner shop instead?" Mum said. "Dont be long, it's nearly dinner-time."

She gave Andrew the money and he went at once. Mum had looked at him in such an odd, searching way that he wanted to get away.

The corner shop was quite near but Andrew had to wait because Mrs Cooper, the owner, was listening to Miss Pritt from the flat next door to Andrew's. She talked on and on so he made a clinking noise with the milk money and plunked it down on the counter. Miss Pritt talked on.

"Cardboard walls, that's what I reckon them flats has got. Hear every sound, you can," Miss Pritt whined.

"How tiresome, dear," said the kindly Mrs Cooper.

"Yes, well, then there's her upstairs with her late baths. Proper unsettlin' it is, all that water gurglin' and slurpin' down the drain last thing at night, like," Miss Pritt went on in her squeaky voice.

Andrew shuffled his feet and coughed. Miss Pritt peered at him through her thick-lensed glasses.

"Aren't you the Miller boy?" she

squeaked. "What's on, then? Are you movin' to one of them new council houses?"

"I don't know. Mum says we're on the waiting list," Andrew replied.

"So I should hope, what with that baby sister of yours and that. Soon be needin' her own bedroom, like. More space, that's what you Millers wants, and a garden to put the pram in."

Miss Pritt's voice became even more shrill as she planned Andrew's new home.

"I'd like a garden," Andrew said.

"Course you would. Your dad should make a right fuss before all them new houses is taken, that's what," Miss Pritt declared.

"You look hot and bothered, dearie. Is anything wrong?" Mrs Cooper asked.

She folded her plump arms on the counter and leaned towards Andrew. She gave him such a warm, motherly smile that he told her the truth.

"I've lost a white rabbit," he blurted out.

"A rabbit! 'Pon my soul!" Miss Pritt squeaked. "Don't mean that Susie's rabbit, do you? If so, how come you lost it, like?"

She peered at Andrew more closely, her beady eyes gleaming with nosiness. He did not stop to explain.

"Can I have a pint of milk, please. Mum's waiting for it," he said to Mrs Cooper.

"Here you are, dearie. All fresh and cool from the fridge," she replied.

"Fancy that, then. Losin' someone else's rabbit. There's a thing!" Andrew heard Miss Pritt saying as he hurried from the shop.

5

The End of the Chase

"I'M taking Lucy to the clinic this afternoon. Do you want to come with me?" Mum asked after dinner.

"No thanks. I don't like all those screaming babies," Andrew replied.

"What are you going to do, then?" Mum wanted to know.

"I'll go to Base Three . . . to Trevor's house, I mean," Andrew said.

Mum gave him a queer look but asked no more questions.

"I'd like you to post this letter to Grandma first," she said.

Out in the sunshine, Andrew was surprised to see Trevor Cummings staring up at the flats.

"You haven't reported to Base Three for briefing on quarry," Trevor mumbled out of the side of his mouth.

"What are you talking about?" Andrew asked.

"You haven't been to my house to ask about the rabbit," Trevor translated his detective talk.

"I saw you cycling in the park and thought you'd given up looking for him," Andrew replied.

"No clues on waste ground so widened field of search," Trevor muttered.

"Why don't you talk properly?" Andrew said irritably.

"What about going to the park now?" Trevor suggested.

"I must post this letter first," Andrew told him.

"Right. While you're doing that I'll have another look for white quarry. We'll both report back to Flat Base, right?" Trevor said.

Andrew posted Grandma's letter, then found Trevor waiting for him outside the flats.

"No clues. White quarry has covered

tracks well," he said.

"Look, this isn't a game. I've *got* to find that rabbit!" Andrew exploded.

"Message received and understood," Trevor said, his freckled face serious for once.

They searched among the bushes in the park but could not find Susie's rabbit. They came to a playing field where Trevor lost interest in the "white quarry" as he called the rabbit. Several boys were kicking a large ball around the field.

"Come on, let's join in," Trevor said.

"No, there's Oswald Chop. I don't play with him. He's a bully," Andrew replied.

"He won't bully Detective Inspector Cummings," Trevor said, and off he ran.

Andrew wandered down a path on his own.

"Even if Susie's rabbit is here, how will I ever find him?" he groaned.

Despair gripped him. The search

seemed so hopeless. Susie would soon be home and he would have to tell her what he had done.

Ahead of him he saw a flower-bed on one side of the path and some wooden seats on the other. A little old lady dressed all in black sat on one of the seats. She was reading a book, holding it close to her face.

A moment later Andrew could hardly believe his eyes. The white rabbit hopped out of the flower-bed and crossed the path to the old lady. He sat up on his hind legs and banged her on the knee, as he had once done to Andrew.

The elderly lady dropped her book and let out a shrill screech. The rabbit ran back into the flower-bed. The big ball landed close by and bounced towards the rabbit.

Suddenly everything seemed to happen at once. Trevor and the other boys raced towards the ball, which Oswald Chop grabbed.

"Trevor, help! There's Susie's rabbit," Andrew yelled.

Trevor became a detective again.

"Listen, everyone," he ordered. "We must catch that white spy for Andrew. You three approach the quarry from over there, you three head him off that way, and Andrew and I will go straight forward."

With so many boys coming from all angles, the rabbit panicked. He bolted straight ahead, the only way of escape.

SPLASH! In his terror the white

rabbit leapt straight into the river flowing through the park.

Andrew and Trevor jumped in after him, knee deep in the swift current. Andrew waded out and grabbed Percy by the neck and lifted him out of the water.

The rabbit kicked and struggled but Andrew held on tight. Trevor helped by gripping Percy's hind legs.

"Don't let him go! He mustn't get away!" Andrew gasped.

Between them they carried the struggling rabbit to the bank. The other boys cheered and helped them out of the water.

"I'll take charge of that rabbit. Give it here," Oswald Chop demanded.

"No! It's my friend's," Andrew yelled, elbowing Oswald away.

"Here, you kids, off this lawn!" an angry park keeper shouted.

All the boys ran back to the playing field, except Andrew and Trevor.

"We had to catch this rabbit. He's my

friend's but he escaped," Andrew explained.

"Take him away then. Off this lawn, quick!" the park keeper said.

They did not need telling twice. Andrew and Trevor hurried away still holding the wet, wriggling rabbit between them.

At last they had Percy safely back in his hutch. Andrew rolled on to the grass and heaved a big sigh of relief.

"Thanks a lot for helping," he panted.

"That's OK. Detective Inspector Cummings glad to be of use," Trevor grinned. "I'm going back to the park to finish that ball game."

Just then Susie ran out of her back doorway.

"Where's my Percy been? And why's he sopping wet?" she asked.

So Andrew told her what had happened.

"It was all your fault! Mummy told you not to take him out of his run," Susie said crossly.

"I'll never do it again," Andrew assured her.

"I'll ask Mummy to rub him dry," Susie said.

Andrew slipped away to the back stairs. He dared not face Susie's mother. Indoors his own mum was in the living room, bouncing the baby on her lap and singing: "Lucy, Lucy, sweet and juicy."

"Where have you been? Your jeans are soaked," she asked Andrew.

"I . . . I fell in the river in the park,"

he replied.

He tried to escape to his own room but his mother called him back.

"Come here. I think you've got a lot of explaining to do," she said.

"Explaining what?" Andrew asked, but he could not look her in the face.

"What's this Miss Pritt told me about a lost rabbit?" Mum prompted.

Andrew could feel his face turning scarlet. So Mum knew! He sat down and told her the whole story.

"But it's all right now. Percy's back in his hutch," he ended.

"All that trouble and all those lies, just because you were disobedient," Mum said sadly. "I shan't punish you because you've been punished enough all day, but I hope you will tell Jesus you are sorry for disobeying Susie's mother and thank him that you found the rabbit in the end."

"I will, Mum. I really do want to follow Jesus and live his way. It . . . it's just that I've made a mess of things today," Andrew replied.

He was glad his mother was not angry with him, but he disliked seeing her look so sad. He would ask Jesus right away to help him to be obedient and truthful.

After tea Dad opened a long brown envelope that had been waiting for him all day.

"Darling, listen to this!" he exclaimed, waving the letter at Mum.

"What?" she asked and she, too, sounded excited.

"The council's offered us a house on the new estate!" Dad said, his face beaming.

"With a garden?" Andrew asked.

"Yes, with a garden," Dad grinned.

"Will you make me a rabbit hutch?" Andrew asked, bouncing up and down on his chair.

"Yes, I'll do that for you, son," Dad promised.

"And we'll buy you a white rabbit for your birthday," Mum added.